W9-ANC-535

RAGS
THE FIREHOUSE DOG

RAGS

THE FIREHOUSE DOG

By ELIZABETH MORTON

Pictures by Morgan Dennis

The John C. Winston Company

PHILADELPHIA · TORONTO

Copyright, 1952, by
THE JOHN C. WINSTON COMPANY

*Copyright in Great Britain and in
the British Dominions and Possessions*

*Copyright in the Republic
of the Philippines*

FIRST PRINTING, OCTOBER, 1952
SECOND PRINTING, APRIL, 1953
THIRD PRINTING, MAY, 1956

Made in the United States of America

L.C. Card # 52-8979

Z-56

To the real Rags

and to
all the firemen
at
Engine Company Number 20
in Philadelphia

Rags was a not-so-little, not-so-big dog with shaggy brown and white hair and with a tail that was not-so-short, not-so-long. But her ears were very big and almost always they stood straight up. The ends of her ears did not stand up, though. They turned over.

Rags lived in the firehouse called Engine Company Number 20. She liked living there.

1

All the firemen were her friends. Tom was her friend, and Sam, and Bill, and Elliott, and Gene, and Jack, and George. Rags liked all the firemen, but Tom and Sam were her favorites. They were the firemen who gave her a nice breakfast of cereal and milk every morning. At night they filled a big bowl full of dinner for her. She had dog biscuits to eat, too, and liver and vegetables and sometimes a spoonful of cod-liver oil. She did not like the cod-liver oil very much, but because Tom gave it to her, and called her a "good dog," she swallowed it.

Rags and her firemen friends were very busy. The firemen swept out the firehouse every day. They cleaned and polished and oiled the hose truck. They had the pumper to look after, too.

The hose truck took the hose to the fire. The pumper was used to force the water from the fire hydrant through the hose so that the firemen could put out the fire. Tom and Sam were called "pump operators" because they were the firemen who tended the water pressure so that the water could reach a very high fire or one that was a long distance from the fire plug.

Rags watched everything. The firemen said

she wanted to be sure they did a good job. They called Rags their mascot. When their work was finished, the firemen romped with Rags. Then she would run around in circles and bark. Everyone had lots of fun.

Rags had other friends, too—the boys and girls who walked past the firehouse on their way to school in the morning, and back home in the afternoon. Mornings, they only called to her. But afternoons, they had time to stop. On nice days, Rags would be sitting outside the firehouse door on her bench when they came along. Then the boys and girls would pat her and call her a good dog. Rags liked that. She wagged her not-so-long, not-so-short tail and wriggled all over, which meant, "Thank you. I like you too."

Sometimes the children said, "Come on, Rags. Get down off that bench and play with us. We'll race you to the corner."

But no matter how hard the children coaxed, Rags wouldn't budge. She knew her duty. Like Tom and Sam and all the other firemen, she had to stay at the firehouse. She had to be where she could hear the buzzer and the voice on the loud-speaker when it called for Engine 20 to go to a fire.

5

The children always hoped for a fire when they were there. It was such fun to watch Rags then. As soon as the buzzer sounded, she would jump down from the bench. Then she would tear through the firehouse door, barking at the top of her lungs.

If by that time the loud-speaker voice was saying, "At-ten-tion Engine 17, At-ten-tion Engine 17," through the door, the children would see Rags turn around and come outdoors to the bench again. They thought this was because Rags understood the words. But the firemen said it was because they weren't running for their firemen's hats and their slickers.

For Rags knew that if they were just sitting still and listening, Engine 20 wasn't needed at the fire.

But if the loud-speaker voice said, "At-ten-tion Engine 20! At-ten-tion Engine 20," what excitement! Rags kept right on barking, and

the firemen didn't sit still any more. They hustled for their firemen's hats and their slickers, ran for their places, and went right on listening to the loud-speaker voice.

The voice was telling them where the fire was. "Box 54 calling . . . Box 54 calling . . . Fire at Sixth and Maple . . . Fire at Sixth and Maple . . ."

No matter how quickly Tom and Sam got to the pumper, Rags was always there first. Tom was the driver. The pumper was very old-fashioned, with Tom's seat on the *right*-hand side. Sam's job was to pull the pumper's bell, and he sat on the *left*-hand side. Rags belonged on the seat between them. The pumper was so old it didn't have any front doors. So when Tom and Sam climbed up to their places, Rags always hopped up right after them.

When Tom drove the pumper out from the firehouse, the children shouted and waved. But Rags paid no attention to them. She was a firehouse dog, and she was on her way to help put out a fire.

With his left hand, Sam pulled the pumper bell. With his right hand, he held onto Rags. This was so that Rags wouldn't fall out when the pumper raced around street corners.

Clang, clang, clang went the pumper bell. When the people on the street heard that, they got out of the way. *Clang, clang, clang!* All the trolley cars stopped to let the pumper pass them. Rags's ears flopped in the breeze and her red tongue hung out. It was very exciting.

8

One day when the fire signal sounded, Rags was out in the parking lot behind the firehouse, romping with another dog. She was having so much fun that when the buzzer went off, she didn't hear it. And she didn't hear the firemen running for their hats and slickers as the loud-speaker voice said, "At-ten-tion, Engine 20," either.

When Tom and Sam reached the pumper, they took a quick look around for Rags. Where *was* she? They couldn't wait to find her. They had a fire to put out. They must get the pumper there as fast as they could.

Out from the firehouse went the pumper, with Tom driving and Sam pulling the bell. Out from the firehouse went the hose truck. *Clang, clang, clang!* Everybody got out of the way. At the busy corner two blocks away, the policeman blew his whistle for the traffic to stop. *Clang, clang, clang!* The pumper and the hose cart raced through the red light.

After the engines passed, the policeman blew his whistle for the traffic to start once more. Then he looked up the street to make sure everything was all right. What on earth was that brown and white streak tearing along, in and out of the line of cars? It was a dog, no doubt about it, ears flapping, red tongue hanging out. Why, it was Rags, his friend Rags from the firehouse!

11

Quickly the policeman blew his whistle
again. Once more the traffic stopped, this time
to let Rags through. On she dashed, with never
a glance at her old policeman friend. On she
dashed, for four blocks more, straight to the
place where Tom and Sam were helping to put
out the fire.

She found the pumper, all right. But when she got there, she was too tired to jump up to her own seat. She just stood on the ground beside the front wheels, panting and gasping for breath. In a few minutes, Tom noticed her there. So he leaned down and lifted her up to her place on their pumper.

There she sat, all the time Tom and Sam were busy. When the fire was over and they were ready to go back to the firehouse, she wagged her not-so-long, not-so-short tail and gave a little bark as if to say, "See, I didn't miss the fire, after all."

One day, after Rags had lived with the firemen for three years, something very unusual happened. A man in a blue suit and a cap trimmed with gold braid came to look at the old pumper. As he walked around, he shook his head.

"She's worn out, all right," he said.

Then he got out a book full of pictures of pumpers. "Look," he said to Tom and Sam and the others. "This is the one they are getting for you. It will come next Saturday. And boy, what a loud siren she has!"

Tom and Sam looked at the picture. "That's fine," they said. "But we're sorry to see the old pumper go."

While the man and Tom and Sam were talking, Rags went out to her bench in the sunshine. No one was there, because all the children were in school. So Rags settled down for a nice nap.

When Tom came to the door and saw Rags sleeping soundly, he said to Sam, "How about my taking Rags home with me for a visit with the twins on Saturday? That's my time off.

I think it will be better if Rags isn't here when they take the old pumper away."

Sam was sad. "That's a good idea," he said, with a sigh, for he too loved the old pumper that had taken them to so many fires.

When Saturday came, Tom and Rags drove off together in Tom's car. When they got to Tom's house, there were Jack and Janey, the twins, waiting for them in the front yard.

"Hello, Daddy," they shouted. "Hi, Rags! You've come to visit us!"

The twins' mother came out of the house to greet them.

"Take Rags out into the back yard, children," she said.

Rags and Jack and Janey had lots of fun in the back yard. The twins threw their ball and Rags ran after it and brought it back. They played tag, trying to catch Rags. Only they never did.

Jack and Janey's mother gave Rags plenty of good things to eat. On Saturday night, Rags slept on a rug on the floor between the children's beds.

Sunday morning, Tom said, "Come on, Rags,

16

old girl. It's time for us to get back to work and see the surprise."

"What surprise, Daddy?" asked Jack and Janey.

Tom winked at them. "You know," he said. "I told you all about it last night."

Then the twins remembered. "Oh, yes, the new pumper. But Rags doesn't know yet, does she?"

17

Tom shook his head. "Not yet. But as soon as she gets back to the firehouse she will."

When Tom and Rags drove up to the firehouse, all the firemen were waiting for them.

"Poor Rags," Sam said. "I wonder how she'll feel."

As soon as Tom opened the door of his car, Rags jumped out. She wagged her not-so-long, not-so-short tail to show how glad she was to be back. Then she hurried into the firehouse to look things over.

Inside the door, she stopped and sniffed. Something was wrong! Something smelled very queer and different! Where was the old pumper? In the place where the pumper belonged stood a thing much bigger and much more shiny. The wheels of this big thing were much larger too. Rags gave a little whine, and looked up at Tom and Sam, who had come up beside her.

"It's all right, old girl," said Tom, leaning down to pat her. "This is our new pumper. It will help put out fires much better than our old one."

"Look, old girl," and Tom opened the front door of the new pumper. "See the fine place where you and Sam and I are going to sit when we go to fires?"

Rags wagged her tail slowly. She could tell by the sound of Tom's voice that he liked this big, new thing. Well, perhaps it was all right. Perhaps . . .

20

Just then the fire buzzer went off. "Engine 20 . . . Engine 20," said the voice over the loud-speaker.

Rags's firemen friends hustled into their hats and their slickers and ran for their places. Tom hopped up into the driver's seat on the left-hand side of the new pumper. Sam ran around to the other side and jumped up beside him. But Rags held back.

"Come on, Rags," shouted Sam. "Come on, old girl. Jump! Here—over here!"

Rags jumped. But as she jumped, something happened! Before Sam could reach out to hold the door open, it had slammed shut on Rags's leg. Even though Sam already had the pumper's siren going, he heard her yelp of pain.

"Hold on, Tom," he cried. "Rags is hurt. Wait a second."

As soon as Tom and Sam looked at Rags's leg, they knew it was broken. "Hey, Jack," Tom called to one of the firemen who was going to stay behind to look after the firehouse. "Rags's leg is broken. Keep her here till we get back. Then we'll take her to the dog and cat hospital."

Tom handed her down gently. And off raced the shiny new pumper out of the firehouse on the way to the fire.

Poor Rags! Never before had Tom and Sam left her behind when she was ready to go. And this time she could not run after them. She couldn't even stand up. Her leg hurt so much

that she didn't even wag her tail when Jack put her down on her old quilt in her special corner.

"You're going to be all right, old girl," he told her. "When Tom and Sam get back, they'll take you to the doctor. I'd take you now myself, only I must stay here to look after the firehouse."

Rags was lying very still, with her eyes shut, when the new pumper and the hose cart came back from the fire. Without even taking off their fire hats and their slickers, Tom and Sam ran out to the parking lot back of the firehouse to get Tom's car.

"Now then, old girl," said Tom, coming up to Rags, "we're going to a nice place where the doctor will make you well."

Then Tom picked Rags up very carefully and put her on the back seat of his car. And he sat on the front seat, holding onto her, as Sam drove to the dog and cat hospital.

When Tom carried Rags inside, a man in a
white coat said, "Come this way, if you please."

The man was the hospital doctor. Tom and
Sam called him the Vet. In a big room that
smelled nice and clean, the Vet took Rags from
Tom's arms and put her on a table. Then he
patted Rags and scratched her behind her ears
and told her she was a good dog. Rags liked the
Vet and did not even squirm when he examined
her leg.

26

"Yes, it's broken," the Vet told Tom and Sam. "But with a splint, it will heal without any trouble. She's in good shape."

Then the Vet put a splint on Rags's leg, and he covered the splint with a long bandage that reached down almost to Rags's shoulder. Rags lay quietly on the table. And when the Vet had finished putting the bandage on, she tried to stand up.

"Take it easy, old girl," said Tom.

"Can she go back with us to the firehouse now?" Sam asked the Vet.

The Vet shook his head. "Better let her stay here at the hospital overnight," he said. "She needs a rest after that accident."

Rags was not happy when Tom and Sam left her. But when the Vet picked her up and took her to a special hospital bed, she settled down like the good dog she was. She liked the Vet. She liked the way he scratched her behind her ears.

But she didn't like the special hospital bed anywhere nearly so well as she did her firehouse quilt. And she was lonely without her firemen friends. All night, whenever a fire engine passed the hospital, she woke up and barked and barked.

The next morning, Rags felt much better, even though her leg was very stiff because of the splint and the bandage. When Tom and Sam came after her, she managed to stand up. The Vet said that was all right. He was glad to see her do it. And he was glad, too, to have her wag her not-so-long, not-so-short tail.

"Let her move around," he told Tom and

Sam. "It will be good for her to do whatever she's used to doing. That's a sturdy splint."

When Tom and Sam and Rags drove up to the firehouse, all the firemen cheered. "Welcome home, Rags, old girl," they said. "Good dog. Good Rags."

As if to join in the welcome, the fire buzzer began to sound. Then the loud-speaker voice said, "Engine 20 . . . Engine 20." Rags wriggled so hard in Tom's arms she almost fell out onto the floor. That was her signal. She was a firehouse dog.

29

"Sure, old girl," cried Tom. "Come on. We three will go to the fire in the new pumper."

Tom put Rags up on the front seat of the new pumper. Then he ran for his firemen's hat and his slicker. Sam got his hat and slicker. And in a jiffy, the three of them were starting off to the fire.

Down one street and up another the shiny new pumper raced. *Wh-ee-e-ee,* went the

siren. And all the people got out of the way. *Wh-ee-e-ee!* All the trolley cars stopped to let the big new pumper pass. Rags's ears flopped in the breeze. Her red tongue hung out. And Sam held onto her tightly so that she wouldn't slip off the pumper's shiny red leather seat when they went around corners.

Soon they reached the fire. It was a very big one in a lumber yard. Many other engines were

there, along with the new pumper and the hose truck from Engine Company Number 20. There were hook and ladder trucks from Company Number 23 and engines and hose carts from other firehouses blocks and blocks away. It was what was called a "five-alarm" fire. That meant that five firehouses had been signaled to help

32

put out the big fire. Everywhere there were
many firemen Rags had never seen before. A
big crowd of people was watching the fire.
Many policemen were helping. They told the
people to keep back and put up a rope to show
the crowd where they must stand.

Tom and Sam jumped down from the front
seat of the new pumper. "Stay right there,
Rags," Tom said.

So Rags stayed on the front seat while Tom and Sam worked the pumper. A big stream of water shot from the hose. "She's a honey, all right," Tom said.

"She sure is," agreed Sam.

Rags watched the fire. For a long time, tall flames leaped up from the wood in the lumber yard. More and more water shot from the hose. Then there were no more flames flickering in the big clouds of smoke. The fire was almost out. After a while, some of the fire engines began to go home. And the Fire Chief came up to look at the new pumper.

While Tom and Sam were talking to the Fire Chief, a tiny little girl toddled out from the crowd behind the rope. She had come to the fire with her mother and father. She was walking around alone because her father thought her mother was holding their little girl by her hand. Her mother thought her father was holding their small daughter by her hand. They did not notice that she had gone away because they were watching the fire engines go by.

But Rags saw the little girl. When the little girl walked right up to the new pumper, Rags

barked and barked. Tom and Sam did not notice Rags's barking because they were on the other side of the pumper talking to the Fire Chief. And no one else paid any attention, either.

Then the little girl walked right under the pumper. That was wrong! A little girl should never go under a pumper! With a very loud bark, Rags got up on her feet.

With her nose, Rags pushed at the pumper door. Slowly the door swung open, and Rags jumped out. When she landed on the ground,

her broken leg hurt very much. But Rags went
right on. She was a firehouse dog. She had a
job to do.

Under the pumper Rags went, then up to the
little girl. The little girl smiled at Rags and said,
"Nice doggy."

But Rags didn't take the time to wag her
not-so-long, not-so-short tail. Getting a good
hold with her teeth on the little girl's dress,
Rags pulled and pulled. The little girl sat down
on the ground and began to cry. But Rags went
right on pulling.

37

Behind the rope, the little girl's mother suddenly missed her small daughter.

"Where is Sally?" she cried to her husband.

"I thought she had hold of your hand," said Sally's father.

"I thought she had hold of yours," said the mother.

In and out among the people near by, they ran and ran, and looked and looked, and called and called. But Sally didn't answer.

"Quick, ask the policeman over there to help us," said Sally's mother.

"Our little girl is lost," the father told the policeman. "Her name is Sally and we can't find her."

The policeman looked over toward the pumper. "There she is," he said. "See, that dog is looking after her."

Sure enough, Rags had pulled the little girl out from under the pumper. There she was, safe and sound, with Rags still holding onto her dress. The mother and father and the policeman ran out to get her. Tom and Sam and the Fire Chief came from behind the pumper to see what all the excitement was about.

A young man with a camera came hurrying up. "Whose dog is that?" he asked.

"She's the mascot of Engine Company Number 20," Tom and Sam said proudly. "Her name is Rags, and she goes to all the fires on our pumper."

"What's the matter with her leg?" the young man asked then.

"It's broken," Tom and Sam told him.

"And she hopped down to make a rescue!" exclaimed the young man. "My newspaper will want to tell all the people in the city about a dog like that. She's a heroine. Now then, I'll take her picture."

The little girl's mother and father agreed that Rags certainly was a heroine. The Fire Chief and the policeman thought so too. When the people behind the rope heard what Rags had done, they cheered. Tom and Sam were very proud.

The young man got busy with his camera. He took a picture of Rags and Sally. He took a picture of Sally's mother holding her small daughter and the father holding Rags. Then the young man asked Tom and Sam to get up onto the seat of the pumper. The Fire Chief himself lifted Rags up to sit between her old friends. And he took off his own Fire Chief's hat and put it on Rags's head. Tom and Sam thought that the best picture of all.

When Rags drove back to the firehouse with Tom and Sam, she was very tired. Her leg hurt and she was glad to have her old quilt to lie on.

But she was very happy. All the firemen of Engine Company Number 20 crowded around her and patted her. They too called her a heroine. Rags didn't know what that word meant. But when they said she was a good dog, she understood that, all right.

It didn't matter that her leg was stiff because of the splint and the bandage. She was a good dog. She belonged to the firemen of Engine Company Number 20, especially to Tom and Sam.